This Book belongs to

Groovy Chick

We hope you enjoyed this book. As we learn and grow, we'd love a rating or review for it on Amazon, if you have time. **Thank You!**

Loads more from Under The Cover Press
available at amazon

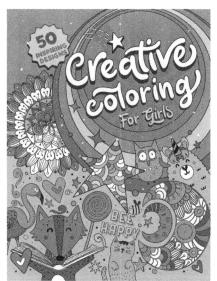

ISBN 979-8575406419

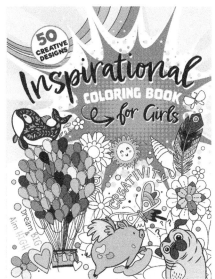

ISBN 979-8430304089

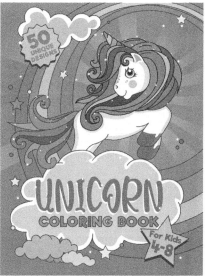

ISBN 979-8695161878

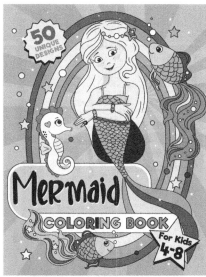

ISBN 979-8484253012

ISBN 979-8590346219

GROWN UPS!
VISIT US AT
UnderTheCoverPress.com

OR SCAN TO VISIT US

• FREE STUFF • NEWS • • INFO •

ISBN 979-8559845876

ISBN 979-8559850436

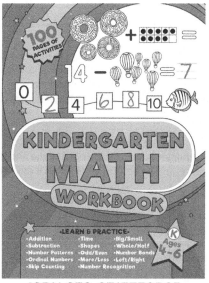

ISBN 979-8717778565

Check out our Toddler coloring series! 100's of big pages filled with coloring
and learning fun. From animals to vehicles, letters to colors and
spooky Halloween to festive seasonal designs... it's got it all!

available at **amazon**

ISBN 979-8552067565

ISBN 979-8509492808

ISBN 979-8520557715

ISBN 979-8522168223

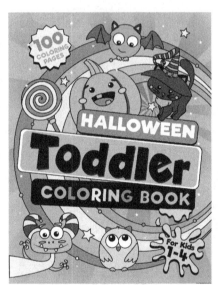

ISBN 979-8548451484

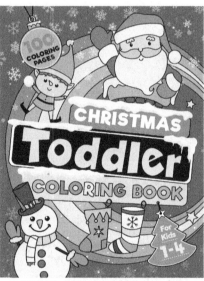

ISBN 979-8473139457

Made in the USA
Las Vegas, NV
03 November 2023

80148862R00059